The Grocery Game

Written by:

Tori Murphy and

Theodora Smiley Lacey

Illustrated by:

Megan Rizzo

To curious children and loving grandparents.

When Grandma and Maya would go to the store,

their conversations were never a bore.

They looked at the veggies, fruits, and meats,

Maya's favorite aisle was the one full of sweets.

"What if" is the name of the game they would play,

as Grandma picked up groceries for the day.

Maya would ask big questions on her mind

and Grandma would answer, so thoughtful and kind.

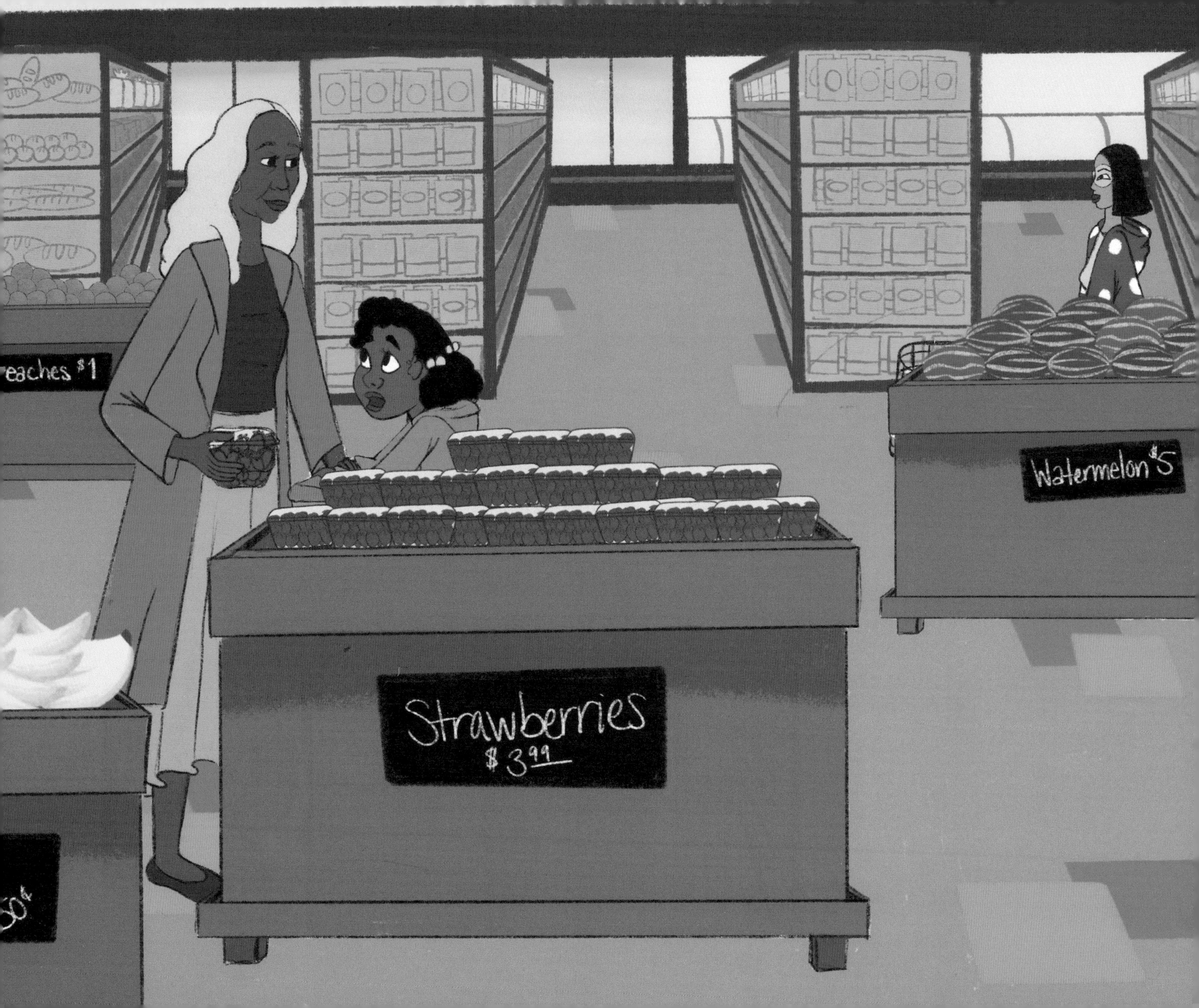
eaches $1
Watermelon $5
Strawberries
$3.99
50¢

What if oaks were the only tree?

There would be no apple, pecan, or redwoods to see.

What if every day were rainy and grey?

No snow, no rainbow, no sunny day

What if the stars didn't twinkle at night?

Think about sailors who follow that light.

What if ice cream were the only food to eat?

What about strawberries, sandwiches, sushi, and other treats?

What if all people in the whole world looked just the same?

You would miss what makes each of us unique, and wouldn't that be a shame?

They walked from the store back to the car,

Maya's mind still buzzing with wonderings of the world both near and far.

Grandma loved the questions Maya shouted out,

"Asking questions is what learning is all about!"

Thinking of their next shopping spree,
Maya couldn't wait. Just Grandma and me.

Published by Stirred Stories

First Edition: May 2020

Tori and Theodora are granddaughter and grandmother who love to read. Theodora is a former teacher who has worked her whole life to make sure that people's voices are heard. Tori is a teacher who cares about creating an environment in which all students feel empowered to be themselves and respect others. Theodora and Tori love going on adventures together and writing this book has been the most exciting one yet!

Megan Rizzo, a proud dog mom and avid gamer, says that art is the central focus in all areas of her life. She is currently a graphic designer in the Bay area, and she teaches children's art classes. Megan says, "I have a need to create art in some way, every day. I create art that brings the feelings of warmth and nostalgia, showcasing people's daily struggles. To me, art is a form of expression; my way of talking to people is through my art."

CPSIA information can be obtained at www.ICGtesting.com
Printed in the USA
BVIW120544270121
598652BV00001B/1